CAN IT BE TRUE?

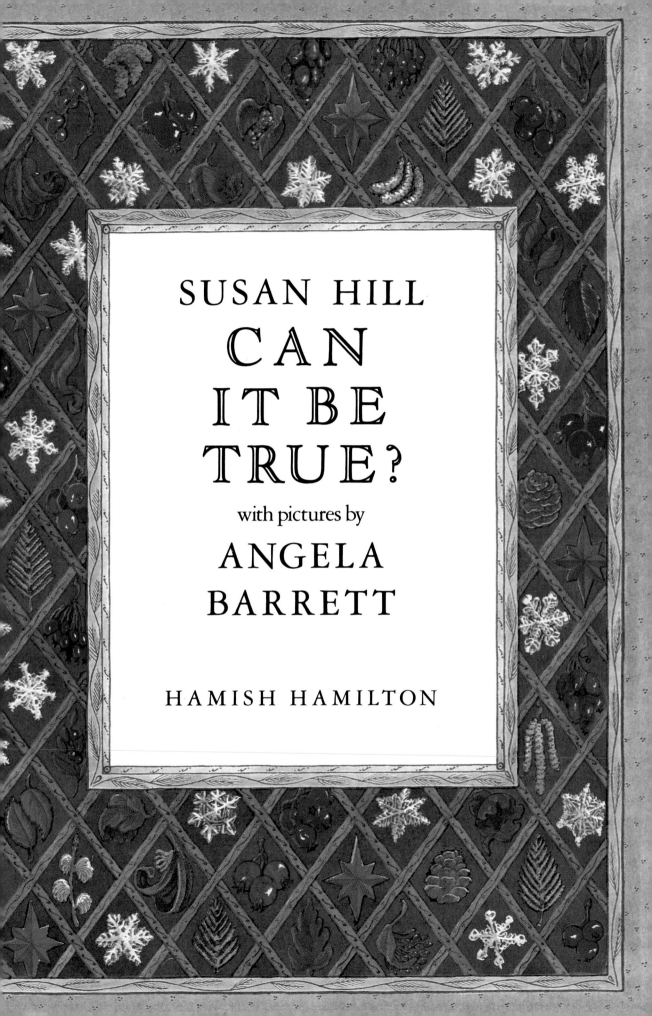

SUSAN HILL
CAN IT BE TRUE?

with pictures by

ANGELA
BARRETT

HAMISH HAMILTON

HAMISH HAMILTON CHILDREN'S BOOKS

Published by the Penguin Group
27 Wrights Lane, London W8 5TZ, England
Viking Penguin Inc., 40 West 23rd Street, New York, New York 10010, U.S.A.
Penguin Books Australia Ltd, Ringwood, Victoria, Australia
Penguin Books Canada Ltd, 2801 John Street, Markham, Ontario, Canada L3R 1B4
Penguin Books (N.Z.) Ltd, 182-190 Wairau Road, Auckland 10, New Zealand

Penguin Books Ltd, Registered Offices: Harmondsworth, Middlesex, England

First published in Great Britain 1988 by
Hamish Hamilton Children's Books
Text Copyright © 1988 by Susan Hill
Illustrations Copyright © 1988 by Angela Barrett

British Library Cataloguing in Publication Data
Hill, Susan, 1942-
Can it be true?
I. Title
823'.914[J]

ISBN 0-241-12155-8
Printed in West Germany

It was Christmas Eve,
on the farm
in the fields
in the streets of the town.

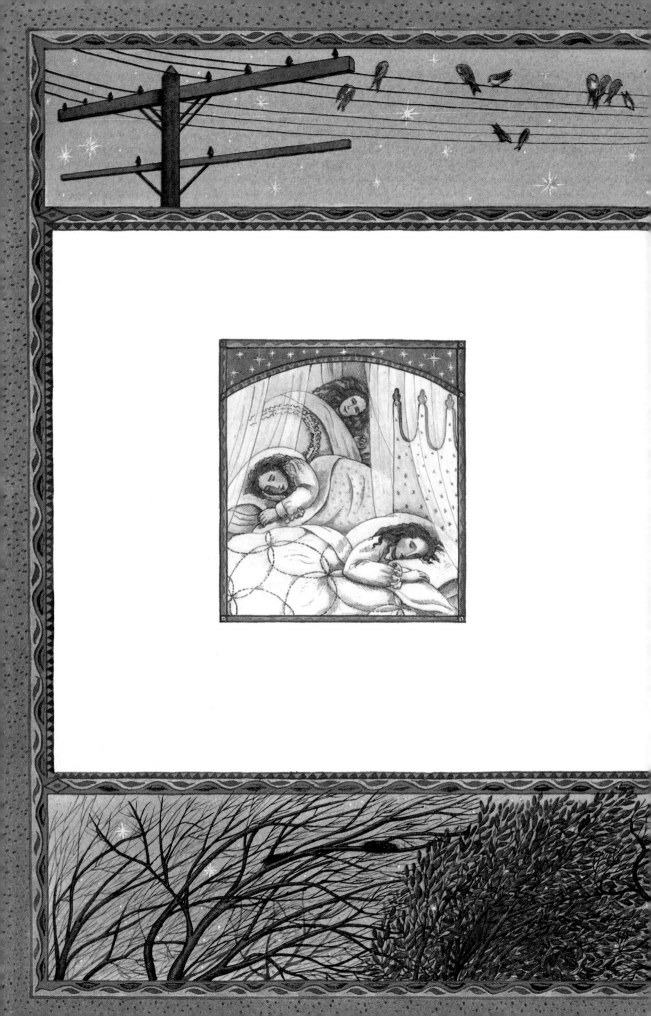

It was Christmas Eve
and twelve of the clock,
when the message was heard
on the wind in the trees
on the air
underground
and humming through wires
and slipped into dreams.

Heard by the fox
slinking up to the hens
in their ark in the dark
and the worm, down, down,
and the wolf as it prowled
near the sheep in the fold.

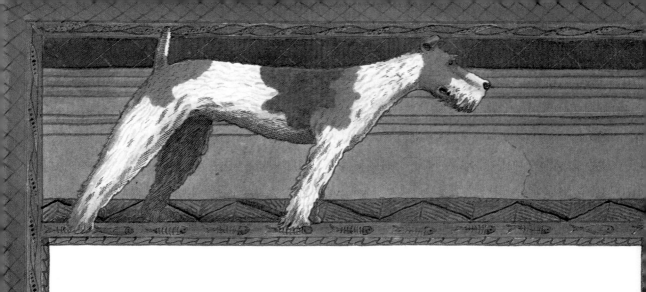

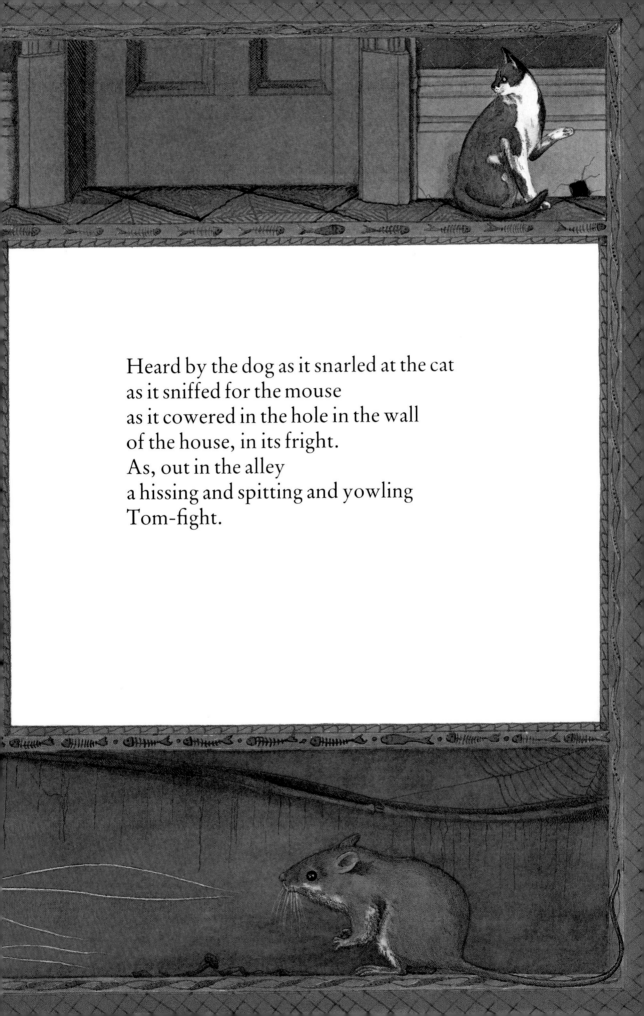

Heard by the dog as it snarled at the cat
as it sniffed for the mouse
as it cowered in the hole in the wall
of the house, in its fright.
As, out in the alley
a hissing and spitting and yowling
Tom-fight.

It was heard by the owl
with blood on its beak,
and the shrew
in the ditch

and the general in bed and dreaming
of war
and the fierce lines of soldiers
on nursery floor.

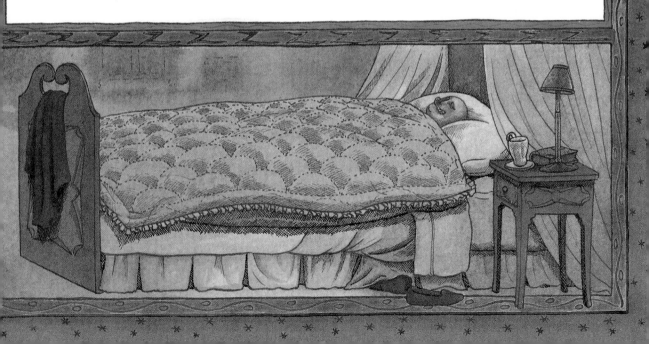

Heard by the weasel,
the ferret, the stoat,
the terrified rabbit
the whale in the sea
and the whaler above in his boat.

And the huntsman,
tantivvy, tantivvy in sleep.
The hounds
and the hare
out there in the fields
where the frost hard as iron held
the earth in its grip.

Christmas Eve and twelve
chimed the clock
on the church
in the town
on the wall
in the hall,
when the message was heard.

Christmas Eve.

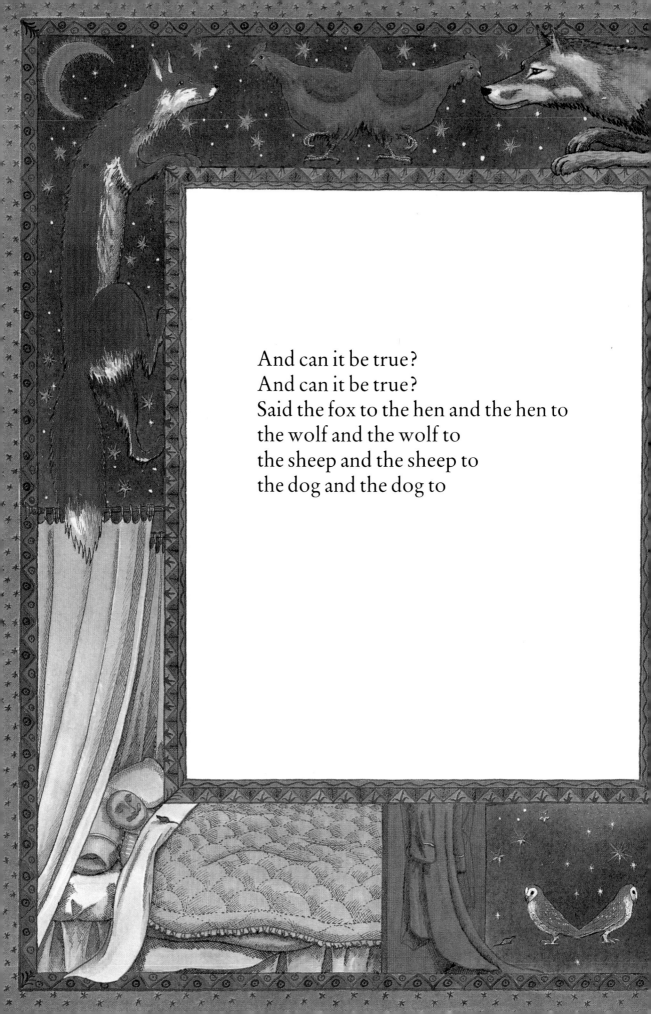

And can it be true?
And can it be true?
Said the fox to the hen and the hen to
the wolf and the wolf to
the sheep and the sheep to
the dog and the dog to

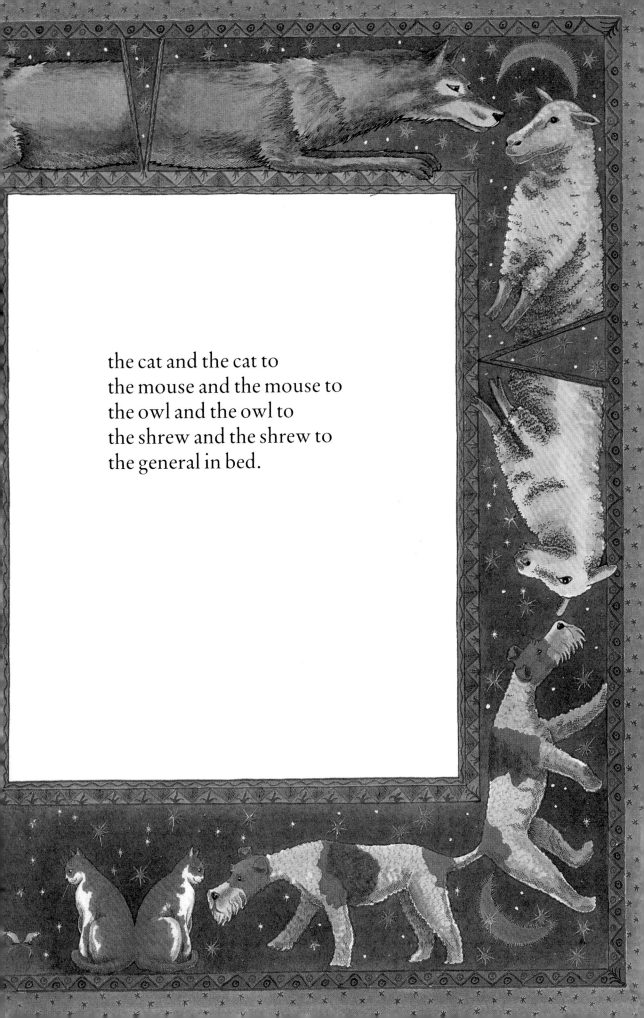

the cat and the cat to
the mouse and the mouse to
the owl and the owl to
the shrew and the shrew to
the general in bed.

Can it be true?
He said
in his dreams to the men in their lines
on the nursery floor, and the men
to the weasel and ferret and stoat,
and the whale to the man
with the gun in his boat.

Can it be true?
said huntsman to hounds,
tantivvy, tantivvy,
and hounds to the hare
in the field
in the cold.

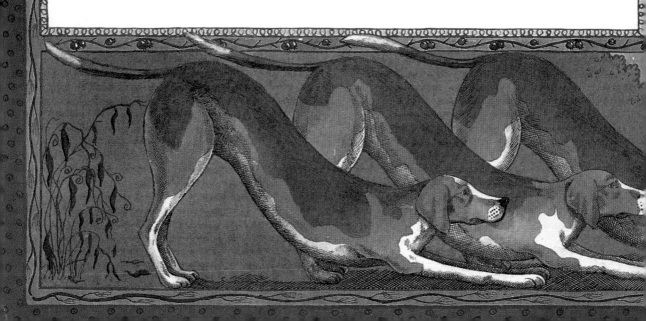

And can it be true?
When the message was heard.
Come and see for yourself.
So they left off their
fighting and hunting and chasing
and dreaming of war.

And they went:
the fox with the hens
and the wolf with the sheep
and the dog with the cat
and the cat with the mouse
and the owl with the shrew

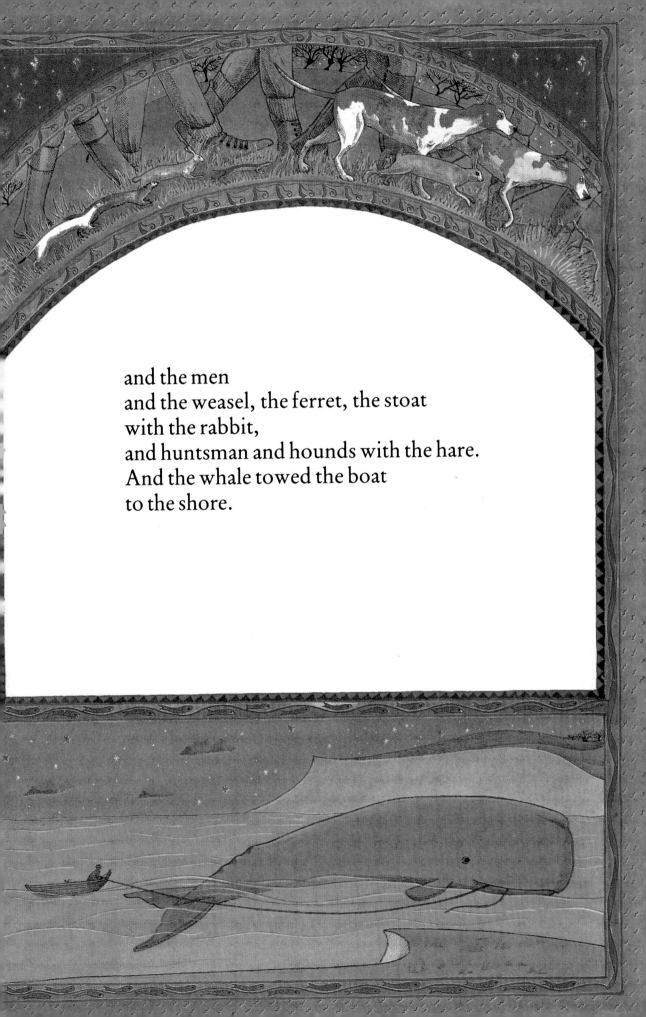

and the men
and the weasel, the ferret, the stoat
with the rabbit,
and huntsman and hounds with the hare.
And the whale towed the boat
to the shore.

And half the way there,
through the fields, and the woods
and the streets of the town
came the snow.

Christmas Eve
and twelve of the clock
when they came to the stable
and saw...

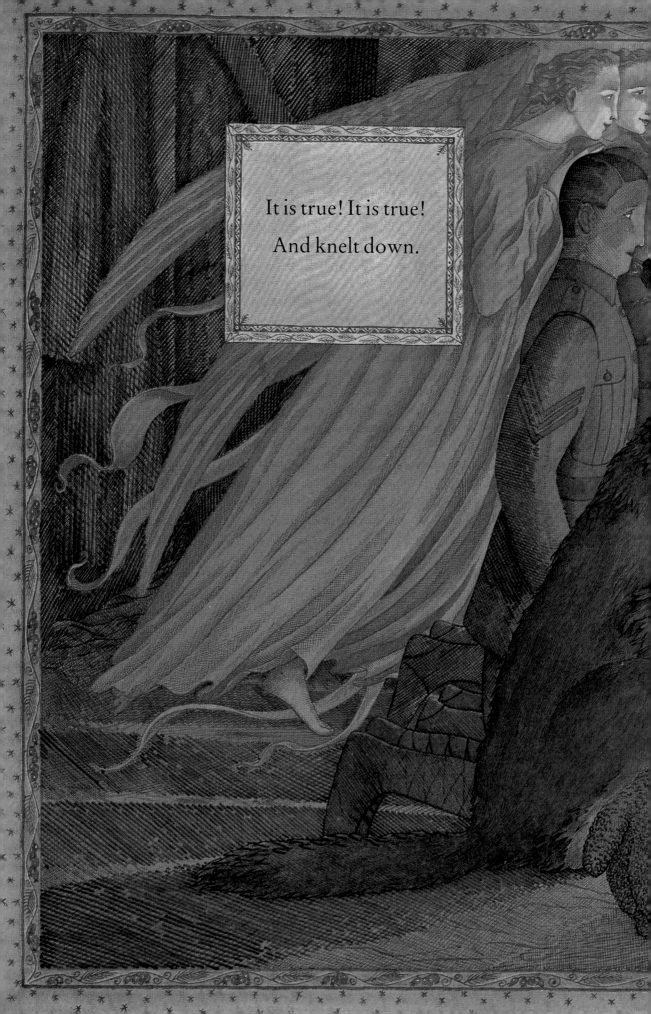

It is true! It is true!
And knelt down.